Little Cloud and Lady Wind

Toni Morrison
& Slade Morrison

ILLUSTRATED BY
Sean Qualls

A Paula Wiseman Book
Simon & Schuster Books for Young Readers
NEW YORK   LONDON   TORONTO   SYDNEY

SIMON & SCHUSTER BOOKS FOR YOUNG READERS
An imprint of Simon & Schuster Children's Publishing Division
1230 Avenue of the Americas, New York, New York 10020
For information about special discounts for bulk purchases, please contact Simon & Schuster
Special Sales at 1-866-506-1949 or business@simonandschuster.com.
The Simon & Schuster Speakers Bureau can bring authors to your live event. For more
information or to book an event, contact the Simon & Schuster Speakers Bureau at
1-866-248-3049 or visit our website at www.simonspeakers.com.

Book design by Laurent Linn
The text for this book is set in Bebop.
The illustrations for this book are rendered in acrylic, collage, and pencil.

Manufactured in China
1109 SCP
2 4 6 8 10 9 7 5 3 1
Library of Congress Cataloging-in-Publication Data
Morrison, Toni.
Little Cloud and Lady Wind / Toni Morrison and Slade Morrison ;
illustrated by Sean Qualls.
p. cm.
"A Paula Wiseman book."
Summary: Little Cloud does not want to join the other clouds in terrorizing the earth with
storms, but grows lonely and longs to look closer at mountains and seas, until Lady Wind
makes her dream come true.
ISBN 978-1-4169-8523-5 (hardcover)
[1. Clouds—Fiction. 2. Winds—Fiction. 3. Individuality—Fiction.] I. Morrison, Slade.
II. Qualls, Sean, ill. III. Title.
PZ7.M8288Lit 2010
[E]—dc22
2008046636

To Safa
—T. M.

To Ford Morrison and his first—Nidal
—S. M.

For Ginger and Selina
—S. Q.

Clouds scattered in the sky. The biggest one said, "Come here, all of you. There is no strength in being alone. We clouds have to stick together if we want to be strong and if we want to terrify the earth with storm and thunder."

The clouds gathered together—all but one. This Little Cloud drifted off by herself. Not wanting to blend into a group and lose her freedom, not wanting to frighten the earth, she found a quiet place in the sky.

Nice as it was in her home in the sky, Little Cloud was lonely. She liked being free but felt sad thinking that all she would ever be was a cloud: soft, drifting, and helpless. From the high place of her home in the sky, she could see such beautiful things down below. Purple mountains with scarves of snow. Valleys full of bright flowers and tall green grass. Silver waves rippling over oceans of ever-changing colors. Little Cloud loved the earth and did not want to join the other clouds to scare it.

"If I could only walk," she said. "Or lie down. Or swim.
I am tired of drifting. I want to touch the earth.

"I want to skip in the snow.

"I want to lie down
with the valley flowers.

"I want to play in the silver-topped waves."

Night came and Little Cloud fell asleep dreaming
of what it must be like to live and play on the earth.
Suddenly she felt a push. Then another. Then
another until she was wide awake.

"Who are you?" she asked.

"I am Lady Wind. I have seen your dream.

Come with me and I can help you."

Lady Wind reached out and took Little Cloud in her arms. Together they raced across the sky.

Suddenly a huge mass of dark clouds appeared, followed by a loud crack of thunder. The ocean leaped and trees in the valley bent low.

"I am afraid," cried Little Cloud.

"Don't be," said the Lady. "Hang on."

All night they flew, chased
by the thunderclouds. They
dodged knives of
lightning, bumped into
mountaintops poking
through the dark, jumped over
ocean waves reaching up to grab them.

Little Cloud held on tight and tucked her head as best she could into Lady Wind's dress. Finally, frightened and too tired to help herself, she fell asleep in Lady Wind's arms.

It was morning when Lady Wind woke Little Cloud.

"Look," she said. "Look down."

Little Cloud looked and saw tiny pearls falling from her clothes.

"What is that?" she asked.

"We call it dew," said Lady Wind.

Little Cloud looked again and saw a necklace of many colors stretching from her place in the sky to the valley.

"What is that?" asked Little Cloud.
"We call it a rainbow," said Lady Wind.

Little Cloud looked again and saw
a trail of baby clouds just like her
floating over the waves.

"What is that?" she asked.

"We call it mist," said Lady Wind.

"Oh," said Little Cloud. "Now I see. I can be me *and* part of something too. I am dew touching the earth.

"I am a rainbow lying in the valley. I am mist playing over the ocean. Thank you, Lady Wind.

"I am me and all the things I dreamed of."

J
E
MORRISON

4/10